TO DRESS A SCARECROW YOU... OLD WORN CLOTHES

PEBBLES
A Pack Rat

Printed in the United states of America   ·J

Prentice-Hall International, Inc., London
Prentice-Hall of Australia, Pty. Ltd., North Sydney
Prentice-Hall of Canada, Ltd., Toronto
Prentice-Hall of India Private Ltd., New Delhi
Prentice-Hall of Japan, Inc., Tokyo
Prentice-Hall of Southeast Asia Pte. Ltd.

10 9 8 7 6 5 4 3 2 1

Library of Congress Cataloging in Publication Data

Miller, Edna.
  Pebbles, a pack rat.

  SUMMARY: A pack rat who finds refuge from the
crows in a scarecrow frightens the local children
when the scarecrow begins creaking.
  [1. Rats–Fiction] I. Title.
PZ7.M6128Pe   [E]   76–8850
ISBN 0–13–655399–0

Prentice-Hall, Inc., Englewood Cliffs, New Jersey

PEBBLES
A Pack Rat

Story and pictures by Edna Miller

To Catherine—librarian, collector

Pebbles, the pack rat, filled his nest with bright and shiny things. A key, a coin, some broken glass, a nail, a scarlet feather. For each thing Pebbles carried off he'd trade a stick or stone.

One night he found a field of corn, not far from his woodland home. As he ran between the rows of corn, searching for new treasure, a giant blocked his way.

"This will scare the crows away!"

Pebbles crouched and waited. The giant didn't move. When Pebbles rattled his tail in warning, the scarecrow only stood and smiled.

Pebbles knew he had nothing to fear.

He gnawed at the scarecrow's tattered boots and climbed to the outstretched arms. High above the tasseling corn he saw a house and barn. People lived in houses. They weren't strange to him. There were many things in houses to trade for sticks and stones.

"The scarecrow must be lonesome . . ."

"What was that noise?"

The old farmhouse had passage-
ways that only a rat could find.
Pebbles searched the quiet house
for all that he could carry. A silver
spoon, a bunch of keys, a brightly
knitted sock. Just when he found
a pretty cup a dog's bark startled
him.

"My socks are gone!"

Pebbles raced back to the scarecrow. The dog chased close behind but wasn't quick enough to see the pack rat disappear.

Safe inside the scarecrow Pebbles slept.
Almost all that he had gathered was in
his straw-filled bed.

"My sock. The scarecrow stole
it!"

"You can't scare me. YOU put
it there."

"Has anyone seen my glasses?"

When Pebbles raided the house again he was careful to make no sound. He traded some twigs for a candle and comb and a stone for some pieces of glass. He carried them past the sleeping dog.

He found a jar of silver coins; he traded
each and every one for a lovely smooth
round stone.

"We didn't take the money."
"The scarecrow took it!"

"My hair ribbons are gone! Someone put a pebble in the box!"

Before the night was over, with ribbons and toys to be hidden away, Pebbles stopped just long enough to taste some sweet young corn. He wanted berries, nuts and bark. He missed his forest foods.

Inside the scarecrow storeroom he re-
arranged his treasures. With grunts and
squeals of pleasure he patted them into
place. The scarecrow shook and wiggled
as Pebbles moved about.

"Did you hear that noise?"

"It MOVED!"

Pebbles was very hungry. He gathered twigs to trade for food. The dog watched Pebbles come and go. He pretended to be sleeping.

Pebbles searched the house for food, but jugs and jars were tightly sealed. The crumbs were swept away. He only took a golden ring with a stone as red as a berry.

"My ring is gone! There's a
pebble in the box!"

"The children wouldn't take those things."

"There must be some other answer!"

As Pebbles hurried to the scarecrow, hungrier than ever, he spied a dish with scraps of food and bones of different sizes.

When he placed the ring on the dish and snatched the smallest bone, the dog sprang wide awake.

Barking savagely he chased the rat back to the scarecrow shelter.

He ripped and tore at the tattered clothes
until everything the scarecrow held
spilled out in a sea of straw and hay.

Pebbles came many times to the split rail
fence but never crossed over again.